The Night

The Night

A Novella

By

Jace Avery

———————————

MAXON PUBLISHING

The Night

Publisher's Note:
This is a work of fiction. Names, characters, places, and incidents either are the product of the author's imagination or are used fictitiously, and any resemblance to actual persons, living or dead, some business establishments, events, or locales is entirely coincidental.

LIBRARY OF CONGRESS CATALOGING-IN-PUBLICATION DATA

AVERY, Jace
Long Before Morning / Jace Avery 1997—
p. cm.
ISBN-13: 978-1522815747   ISBN-10: 1522815740
1. Contemporary Gay Life—Fiction. 2. Mystery—Fiction.
3. Gay Sexual Relations—Fiction. 4. Contemporary Gay Youth
Relationships—Fiction. I. Title
Printed in the United States of America
Set in Palatino Linotype — Book Designed by Wilson Rushbrook
Final Proofreading by Gabriel Williamson

10 9 8 7 6 5 4 3 2 1

For Roxa. Rest in peace baby girl.

1

I woke up in my car, unable to remember anything I did the night before. My phone was blaring my punk-rock ringtone, notifying me that my best friend was calling.

"Dude, where'd you go last night?" His voice betrayed his concern.

"Honestly, I have no effing clue. I just woke up in my car." I said, hoping he would drop it at that.

"Seriously? You didn't even drink a beer when you were here. You just kind of disappeared around midnight."

"Yeah, I have no idea. I don't remember anything from after I got to your house. Hell, I don't even know where the hell I am."

"Any road signs nearby? Or anything?" His voice lowers to a whisper, the way it does when he is watching a murder mystery on T.V.

"Uhm....let me back out of this clearing. I think I'm by a freeway." I started my car and pulled out easy enough, then I turned onto I-75, discovering I was not that far from Toledo, Ohio. *Oh, hell*, I thought.

"Uh...somehow I made it near Toledo. I'll be back in a few hours, I guess..." My voice trailed off.

"Dude, you musta had one hell of an adventure last night. Later!" He hung up on me.

My name is Drew. And, I guess since I have a four hour drive to my hometown of Ashland, Kentucky, I should tell you more about myself. I just turned twenty-two years old and finally moved out of my parents' basement into a small, perfect-for-one apartment. My best friend's name is Sam and he just celebrated his twenty-first birthday. The party was last night, and I guess I ditched after a while. I had this girlfriend for a time, but she left me just last month. I had bought her this really pretty engagement ring, and was planning on proposing, but she decided to interrupt my "little speech" to say, that after four years of being together, she no longer loved me. Then she walked out of the restaurant, and out of my life. I was devastated.

Anyway, Sam wanted me to "get out there" again and dragged me along to his blowout party — you know, his first time being able to legally drink — and get so drunk that he couldn't remember who he had even hit on. I wanted absolutely nothing to do with it, but seeing as he is my best friend, and it <u>was</u> his birthday, I went along with it.

Oh crap, I was supposed to take that exit. I got so wrapped up in talking about everything, I wasn't paying attention. Okay, I'll just turn around here, and go back Easy!

I turned around and headed back, going the extra two miles just to be sure that I wouldn't miss my exit again. I turned onto the correct exit and made my way down the stretch of road to my hometown. As I pulled in to the closest parking lot, which happened to be a McDonald's, I saw something odd in the alley between the restaurant and an older building. My curiosity got the best of me, so I decided to investigate.

The scene I came across was more terrifying than any movie I'd ever seen. Blood splattered up the walls of the alley. Blood oozing from the back corner. My heart rate exploded as I inched closer to the source. A body, half covered by trash, laid there, arms and legs splayed as far as they would go. The victim was lying face down on the pavement, slashes going across her back, cutting deep into her skin. I tried holding my breath as I flipped her over, hoping to some higher power that I didn't know this girl. No such luck would come my way. It was my ex-girlfriend, Isabelle, the girl I had hoped to marry.

Her chest looked like someone had tried to thrust a flag pole into it; her stomach was in even worse condition, like an animal had ripped away the flesh and muscle, leaving me a surgeon's view of her organs. Her eyes seemed to be pleading with her killer, trying to figure out why her.

I pulled my phone out and called 9-1-1. I told them what I knew, which wasn't much, and waited for the cops to show up. I gave two officers my report and offered to help them with anything they needed. Then stayed around until they loaded Isabelle into the back of the truck and slowly headed to the morgue. Something in me compelled me to wave good-bye to the girl I loved. In that moment I vowed to figure out who had done this to her.

My mind wandered on my way home from the murder scene. I could not shake Isabelle's pleading eyes out of my mind. It was as if she knew her killer.

I shuddered at that. She really was a sweet girl, and never could have made someone so angry that they would resort to doing something like that to her. I entered the drive of my building, and absent mindedly got out of my car. I knew I'd be seeing more of her in my dreams tonight. I brewed a cup of tea to help soothe myself; enough that I would be able to lie down and go to sleep.

Like *that* would happen.

2

creams filled the air around me. Something wet was running down my hand. The night was dark, and the air was thick. I could taste the copper — blood — and I cannot say that I do not love it. And then, I am running. Nothing is chasing me, except for my own madness. The river is up ahead. Maybe I will just clean off my hands there and go for a drive. Just to clear my head...

I startle awake, panting as if I really had been running. *Something was just not right about that dream. For one, it felt way too real. And it was way too creepy to have been one of my dreams. Maybe it is just how my body is reacting to having found Isabelle last night.*

I jumped in the shower to scrub myself clean of that miserable dream. After I toweled off I checked my phone to find that Sam had called twice to check up on me. I hit his number and waited for him to answer.

"Drew, man. Why didn't you come over last night? I started to worry about you." He yawned through this, leading me to believe I woke <u>him</u> up.

"I uh…ran into some trouble last night." I slowly got the words out.

"What trouble?" I had piqued his interest.

"I came across Isabelle…" My voice trailed off as I remembered the state she was in.

"You didn't get back with her did ya?" His tone sounded like my mom whenever I got into trouble as a kid.

"No. I found her body in an alley. It was so bad, Sam. Who could do something like that to her? I just don't get this." My voice cracked.

"What the fuck?! Oh man! Did you call the cops?! Wait, stay there! I'll be over in a few!" He hung up. *Great, I just know he'll ask me every detail. How I found her, what she looked like, and definitely how much blood there was.*

"Dude! Okay. So did you report it?" He demanded as he barged in, not bothering to knock.

"Yeah, it was brutal, dude. I still can't believe anybody would kill her." I bit my lip, trying hard not to burst from emotion.

"Oh man. How bad was it?" His voice cracked.

"Organ revealed-bad That's how bad." I looked away; up at the ceiling, trying to hold it together, hoping that my mind would never show me her destroyed body again.

"Poor Isabelle. She had her whole life waiting for her." He let his voice drop to a whisper.

"Yeah, I know. I'm just glad I'm not the one who's gotta tell her folks that their daughter was killed." I could feel the first of many tears run down my cheek.

"I'm so sorry Drew. I know you really loved her."

"I still do. Always will." I snapped sharply. I regretted it immediately. It was not very often that I snap like that at my best friend. And like always, it left me feeling like crap. "I'm so sorry about that Sam…" I said softly. "It's just that this whole thing is totally messing with me. I mean, I wanted to marry her, and a month after she leaves me, I find her dead? It's just not adding up in my head." I would hope that little fact wouldn't add up to the detectives, either.

"It's okay Drew. I know you didn't mean to snap at me." He lifts his head and smiles at me, our old sign of everything being truly okay. "You know Drew, I've had this thing for you for a while now…"

Oh man, do not tell me my best friend is going to hit on me right now. "Uh Sam…that's cool and all but…" Next thing I know, his lips are on mine and I am (surprisingly) not trying to pull away. I allow myself to relax and kiss him back, pulling him toward my lap. *This is not happening…*

"Drew…" He's trying to get his breathing under control, "I'm sorry. I shouldn't have done that. Not with everything that's going on. I just don't want you to be upset." He lowers his head again, blushing slightly. I have never been attracted to other men, but somehow this just seems right.

"Shhh, Sam it's okay. Just let me figure this stuff out, and then maybe we can try. We've always been a little closer than best friends are. Just let me figure out the stuff with Isabelle." I know I sound like I'm pleading with him, and maybe I am. But I really do need to figure things out. Not just the Isabelle stuff, but the whole kissing my best friend thing as well.

"Okay Drew, I can do that." He looks up and kisses my cheek, blushing more as he realizes he is in my lap.

"Sorry, heat of the moment." I blush and look away. He climbs out of my lap and goes for the door.

"I'll catch you later, Drew." His voice hints at melancholy, making my chest hurt.

"Sam, wait. You don't have to leave. It was just bad timing. Let's hang out and get a pizza. Just like old times. I'll figure out the Isabelle thing and then we can see where things go." I tender a smile and hope Sam will accept my offer.

"Okay. Want me to call it in?" He asks trying to disguise the obvious happiness laced through his silky voice.

"Yeah, mind if I go take a quick shower?" Normally, I'd never ask such a question in my own home, but Sam is known to be impulsive at times.

"Go for it. I'll find a movie to put in, too." He pushed me towards my bathroom and took off for the living room, giggling like a school girl. I grabbed a t-shirt and a pair of boxers from my bedroom and took the quickest shower of my life. I got dressed and joined Sam in the living room just as the bell rang.

"Andrew Potter?" A stern voice asked as I opened my door to three officers.

"Yes? How can I help you?" I replied coolly.

"May we ask you some questions?" A female officer asked.

"What about? If it's about the girl who was murdered I don't know anything more than I already told you." Anger was starting to build inside me. Sam quietly moved near as a buffer just in case I lost my temper.

"We just need to know how you knew Isabelle." Her voice remained calm.

"I dated her for four years. If that's all, you can go now." My jaw clenched and Sam put his arm around me in a display of protection.

"Calm down, Potter. We don't intend to make this any harder than it already is. When was the last time you saw her alive?" The third officer asked, his voice indifferent.

"The day she walked out of my life over a month ago. Now, please leave." I stormed away, leaving Sam to deal with the cops. *Why'd they have to come now? Everything was going great, and now I'm all mixed up. Ugh!* I slammed my bedroom door shut and threw myself onto my bed.

Sam knocked on my door and stuck his head in. "Pizza's here bud. Let's eat and watch a movie. Then we'll figure it all out together." He walked over to me.

"Yeah, okay. I'm just feeling a lot right now and I'm a little confused." I whispered, trying to maintain some of my machismo.

"I know, Drew. We'll take it one step at a time. First step: pizza." He pulled me out of my bed and into the living room. I sat on the couch and stared at the television screen.

"Here, take this." Sam handed me a plate of pizza and a glass of vodka. My best friend knows exactly just how to take care of me.

"Thank you." I took it from him and continued to stare at the screen. My mind would not stop replaying her walking out of my life.

"Drew, did you hear me?" Sam asked, his face contorted in concerned confusion.

"Uhm…no. I'm sorry…" I lowered my head and my voice. *He deserved so much better than what I could ever give him.*

"I asked if you were okay, but now I can see that you clearly aren't. Try eating your pizza. It'll help." He put his own plate down and moved closer to me.

"Yeah, it'll help." I looked down at my plate and burst into tears. Sam put his arms silently around me after moving my food and booze. I moved my head to his shoulder as I released everything I had kept inside since she had left.

3

I looked down at the blade in my hand. It was streaked with blood and tissue. I smirked as I heard a series of whimpers from below me. Poor little thing never had a chance. I gave a snide chuckle and walked away.

I awoke in Sam's arms, my face wet with tears and sweat. I noticed that he was still sleeping. I carefully moved off of him, as not to wake him. He was so peaceful when he slept. I washed my face a little before heating up some pizza. The floorboards creaked. Sam had gotten up and came over to me. I smiled at his endearing bed head hair.

"Hey, you feeling better?" He asked sleepily while grabbing for my pizza.

"Well enough to tackle you if you steal one crumb." I grinned, as I pulled it away from him.

"Okay, I'll just warm up my own, then. Who needs your stinky old pizza?" He rattled around the kitchen and punched in the numbers on the microwave. "Hey, we kinda missed the entire movie." He smiled, obviously pleased that I was feeling better.

"That's okay. We can start it up again. Besides, it was obvious that I needed to...you know."

"What, be a crybaby?"

"Yeah, that, smartass. Thanks for everything you've done to help me through this, Sam. You truly are my best friend." I hugged him tightly, just like when we were kids.

"Anything for you, Drew. You mean everything to me. And I get it if you don't wanna risk our friendship by trying anything...new. It's cool. I just wanted you to know how I feel, and that I've felt this way since our freshman year."

"Why didn't you tell me sooner?" I blurted out thoughtlessly.

"I didn't want you to think differently of me. And then you got with Isabelle, and now all this is going on."

"Sam, I would never think differently of you!"

"Yeah, you say that but..."

"You're my best friend. You've always been there for me, ever since we were kids. That's not gonna change just because you like me. Not unless *you* let it change. I just wish you would've told me before now, that's all." I pulled him closer—which didn't seem possible—and I held him to my body. I gathered a deep breath, breathing in his scent and wondered how I'd not noticed the fact that he was madly in love with me.

"Drew, I love you so much; as a brother, best friend, and even a potential partner. And I will not lie and say that I hope we won't get together, because I do. More than anything in the world. But I don't wanna lose you from my life if things don't work out." Now he was the one whimpering. I gazed into his eyes.

"Sam, I'd never walk out of your life willingly. Do you understand me?" I kissed him softly and unexpectedly. I was just rolling with everything. And for once, everything seemed right. "I love you Sam, maybe not as a partner yet, but more than just as a brother and best friend, that's for sure."

"I understand, Drew," he said, biting his lip nervously. "Can we just go watch the movie now?" He asked with a quiver in his voice.

"Yes we can." I let go of him and we did exactly that.

Sam left three hours ago. We did not kiss again, and hanging out the way we used to didn't seem weird at all. Now I have to figure out the stuff about Isabelle, and what my recent dreams could mean. This is so conflicting, I want to know, but at the same time I do not. It is ten p.m. and I'm trying to think rationally about all of this. Maybe I just need to go to bed.

4

I looked down at the creature whimpering at my feet. The black of night makes it hard to see anything but the glimmer of the blood. I take in a deep breath, also taking in the metallic scent of its blood. I move a few trash bags over the creature's body, my hands stick with the blood of my victim. I chuckle to myself, feeling a slight hint of pride over my kill. Ha! That will teach it to mess with me.

I awakened with a start. I looked at the clock only to find out it was only two a.m. These dreams are getting to me. Isabelle, why did it have to be my Isabelle? I took in another deep breath, and allowed myself to get up. Maybe sleeping over at Sam's place will help.

I send him a quick text, even though he is sleeping, so he won't freak out in the morning. I pack up a few things and toss my beat up overnight bag into my car. On the drive over, all I can think about is how conflicted I feel. Kissing Sam, when the girl I love had just been murdered. *Does it make me a bad person to want to be with him, when I should be grieving over her?*

I pulled into his driveway and turned off the car. I closed my eyes and remembered the way he smelled when I hugged him. It was intoxicating, but not at all overwhelming. *Am I developing a thing for him when she has only been gone for two days?* I shook the thoughts from my mind and grabbed my overnight bag from the back seat and let myself into Sam's cozy little house. Going straight for the spare bedroom, I dropped my bag on to the floor and flopped onto the bed. *God, it's great to not be alone.* I let my eyes close and my mind drift.

"Drew! Get your very cute butt out of bed!" Sam's voice woke me from a deep, dreamless sleep.

"I'm coming, chill out!" I dragged myself out of the rack and stumbled to the kitchen for some toast.

"You okay man?" He asked, coming around the corner of the dividing wall.

"Yeah, just had some odd nightmares and didn't feel safe staying alone at my place," I yawned, my hand reaching for the bread.

"Dude, I made breakfast. Go sit on the couch. The T.V. tray has your plate and some orange juice," he grinned. What would I do without him?

I sat down, pulling my tray closer to me. I looked at my plate, thinking about how amazing my best friend is. Bacon, eggs, toast, and orange juice sat there before me, all of my favorite things for morning consumption. "Thanks, Sam. It looks amazing!" I took a bite of bacon and eggs. It was like a taste of heaven.

"No problem. When I saw your text, I knew you'd must've had a rough night. I thought maybe having some tasty favorites would help." He shrugged and sat down next to me with his own plate.

"Yeah, it does help. You are a genius." I smiled. We ate the rest of our breakfast in silence. I was too focused on my food to hear anything he could have said anyway. After our breakfast was over, Sam put on a movie and cuddled up to me. I smiled and pulled him closer. No words were exchanged, just our body heat and a handful of smiles as the movie played. My mind drifted over to the nightmares I'd experienced since finding her body. It was as if I was witnessing her being killed, but there was no one else there. None of this was making sense to me, unless I was her killer. But why would I kill her, and then not even remember it?

"Drew, are you okay?" Sam's voice tugged me back to reality.

"Yeah, just started thinking about my nightmares." I looked away, hoping he wouldn't question me any further.

"Okay. If you want to talk about 'em, I'll sure listen." His voice cracked with concern.

"I know Sam. I promise I'll come to you first if I need to talk." I smiled.

"I know, Drew. Just don't shut me out completely, please."

"I won't. I promise." He was so cute when he worried about me. I looked at my phone. Oh crap, time for work. "Hey Sam, I gotta go!"

Sam pouted. "But why? I don't want you to!"

"I know. But I have work. I'll come back as soon as my shift is done. I promise." I softly kissed his forehead.

"Okay, bye, Drew." He was disappointed, but I desperately need to get to work. I need a distraction, anyway. Yes, Sam distracts me pretty well, but I need a clean distraction so I can think about what I want with him, as well as what to do about Isabelle and my odd fricking dreams.

My office is a tiny little room in Dr. Crown's office. Dr. Crown is Ashland's leading dentist, and sadly I work at the receptionist's desk. I'm not a receptionist; not really. I'm the odd job, catch-all guy. In other words, I clean all of the equipment; make sure files are up to date; and yes, do the receptionist work. Even though Dr. Crown is the leading dentist here, our days are usually slow, which means I have plenty of time to think about everything.

I started a list about the dreams and how they were seemingly progressing towards insanity. And that whole 'realistic' feeling thing was really starting to creep me out beyond all explanation. It was almost as if my hands are really sticky with blood when I wake up. I don't understand it. Maybe Sam can help me figure it out later.

Speaking of Sam, what am I going to do about what is going on with us? Kissing him is amazing, and I definitely want to do it again. I'm just not sure it is the best decision right now. I really am developing feelings for him, though. I won't lie, it scares me a lot. I mean, the last person I fell for is now dead way before her time. I can't risk that ever happening to Sam. He's my best friend; he's my best...everything. If he dies, I don't know what I'll do.

Then again, maybe the risk will be worth it. He could be the one who completes me in every way. I guess I really just need to talk to him.

"Drew, it's five-thirty. You can leave for the night." Dr. Crown called from his office.

"Thank you, sir. Good night." I replied, as I shut down my computer and left the claustrophobic confines of the office. I can't wait to get back to Sam's house. To cuddle up to him and relax would be heavenly right now. I quickly made my way back to his place.

"Sam, I'm back!" I yelled, as I opened the door. His steps were quick and loud as he approached me.

"Drew! I missed you. I have something for you! Come with me." He pulled me towards his bedroom to reveal a collection of massage oils, a handful of candles, and a few scattered rose petals.

"Oh, Sam. You really shouldn't have done this. You're amazing!" I softly kissed him and let him remove my shirt.

"Go lay down. You're way too stressed about all of this." He whispered almost seductively as he pulled away from the kiss.

"Mmm, yes sir." I laid on his bed after removing my pants and boxers. My back had been turned to him as I removed my boxers, and I covered myself with the sheet before turning to lay down.

I closed my eyes as he opened a bottle of oil. My muscles were already starting to release the tension, and he had not even touched me yet. I relaxed as he began rubbing the oil onto my back. The stress was quickly leaving my body as Sam worked his magic. I remained still as he made his way down my back. Actually, it was not until his hand brushed my butt that I made any more noise or movements at all.

"Sam…that is my butt…" I nervously got out.

"I know, Drew. Just relax. I know how to behave myself. Not to mention, the butt is a really big stress area." He silenced me. I forced myself to relax as he professionally massaged the oils onto my butt. I was getting a little more nervous as this continued. My heart rate was spiking, and then suddenly, his hands were no longer on my body.

"Sam, where'd you go?"

"Flip over. I'm just getting some more oil, one that won't take forever to get out of your hair if I massage your head." His voice remained steady. I complied, and flipped my body over. I noticed his shirt had disappeared, and his chest looked

31

extremely toned. I decided to close my eyes so I could not only relax more, but also behave myself better. His fingers touched my forehead gently, and I sighed happily as he began to rub my temples. This was the definition of heaven.

As his hands moved down to my shoulders and chest, I snuggled in to a more comfortable position, letting my muscles relax even further. As his hands reached my stomach, I giggled, as I am very ticklish. Something brushed my lips at this time, and I instinctively opened my eyes. I immediately closed them when I realized it was his mouth, and I gave him what he wanted, complete submission. The kiss deepened and he laid on top of me. I moaned softly and wriggled under him playfully, fully aware that the only thing keeping us from having two naked bodies on top of one another, were his sweatpants and the sheet.

His kisses got needier, like he could not get enough of my mouth and my taste. He started biting at my lip, making me moan in response. I definitely wanted this, and it was obvious that he did too. He moved slowly, getting off of me, causing me to open my eyes. He watched my expression change as he lowered his sweatpants. My eyes began to resemble those of a deer caught in headlights as he came back over to me. My heart rate spiked again, resembling the bad beat of disco music.

"Drew, I want you." His words were to the point. He knew exactly what he wanted.

"I can see that, Sam. You're not exactly hiding that." I gestured towards his pelvic region. "But I want you too." I slid over so he could slide in to the bed. His eyes never left mine until we kissed again. My hands moved to their proper place, one on his shoulder, almost around his neck, and the other in his hair. This all seemed right, not taboo as we grew up to believe about gay love making and sexual relations between best friends being. His mouth moved to my neck, and I bit my lip to keep myself quiet. Love bites are my weakness in bed.

He kissed his way down my body, stopping just before my member. He glanced up, silently asking for permission. I nodded, and he began, not taking his eyes off of mine. I moaned as his tongue flicked over the slit of my member. He got my unintentional hint, and continued to tease me with this until I was at the brink of my orgasm. One hand was gently massaging my balls, the other on my butt. My moans grew louder and closer together as he toyed with me. "Sam, I'm gonna cum..." It was barely a whisper, but he heard it, speeding up and pushing my member into his throat. I grabbed the sheets as I exploded in his mouth, my moans almost animal like. As my member shrank back down in his mouth, he cleaned if off. Once satisfied with it, he came back up and kissed me hard.

"How was it?" he asked grinning.

"Best I've ever received." I grinned back. He kissed me again, pulling me on top of him. His kiss was gentle; giving me more recovery time than any girl I have ever been with or ever had. He slowly pulled his lips from mine, and gave me a loving smile. This is it, we really are going to do this. I smiled back.

"Drew, there is a bottle of lube under the stand, and a box of condoms in the stand drawer. Can you get them for me?" His voice was low, still containing its normal silkiness.

"Of course." I reached over in to the stand first, pulling out a condom. Surprisingly my heart rate did not spike like before. I placed the condom on the bed and grabbed the lube from under the stand, giving both to Sam.

He opened the condom and put it on himself. He then applied the lube to his newly wrapped member and my hole. "This will hurt at first. I will be as gentle as I can be, I promise." His voice was gentle as he said this. I nodded, and he lined himself up. I tried to remain relaxed, knowing that if I did not, it would hurt worse. He slowly pushed the head in and stopped, allowing me to get used to it. I bit my lip and nodded, giving him the signal that it was okay to continue. He pushed in a few more inches and waited. We repeated this until he was fully inside me. No longer feeling pain from it, I kissed him passionately. He slowly started to thrust in and out, increasing speed every few thrusts. I moaned softly as he grunted in pleasure.

We spent the last two hours like that. When we finished, Sam told me that I had been his first. I felt a surge of pride take over. Sam fell asleep after I cleaned him up. It was the most amazing sex I have ever had. I am on the verge of passing out, next to my best friend and hopefully my new boyfriend…

5

All I can hear is laughter as the creature gasps for breath, a completely mad laughter, almost resembling that of the Joker's. I look down at my victim, seeing that its head is turned. I notice the face is one that I know. A girl, and her head is next to a puddle. I look in, and my own reflection stares back at me.

I jump out of bed, stifling a scream. Oh god, no. Please tell me these are just nightmares. Deep down I know it all finally makes sense. The night I do not remember, waking up in my car. Being four hours from home, and the nightmares. I killed Isabelle. I look over at Sam, sleeping next to me. I have to leave before I accidently hurt him the way I hurt her. I get out of bed and find my clothes. I grab my bag from the spare bedroom and quietly leave. I will not do that to him. This is for his protection.

I start my car, and pull out of his drive as fast as I can. I hurry home, barely able to see through the tears. There is a police card taped to my door. I am almost certain that they figured it out too. I make the decision to go on the run. I pack all of the cash I have, which is almost two thousand dollars, and a handful of clothes. I leave my apartment and drive as far as I can before the sun comes up.

"Drew?" Sam's voice is frantic as I answer my phone.

"Sam, I had to leave. You would not understand." My voice cracked as I choked back tears.

"Try me." He is pleading with me.

I swallow hard. "Sam, I did something bad that night."

"I don't care, Drew. Please come back or tell me where you are so I can come get you." He is crying now.

"Sam...I killed her..." I choke out as the tears flood my face. "I cannot be around you. I do not want to risk doing it to you too." I hung up on him. I fell for him, made love to him, only to turn out to be the one who killed Isabelle. I lay in the cheap bed I paid for and cried myself to sleep. I woke up to six missed calls and four texts from Sam. I listened to the voice mails. I had broken his heart. I sent "I am sorry. Bye…" in a text message. I hope one day he can forgive me.

My little room above the bar suddenly seemed too small. I went downstairs and ordered a burger and a basket of fries. I sat down at a small table near the door and waited. A flash of color caught my eye and drew my attention to the door. Sam walked in. How did he find me? I lowered my head as my food came over. I thanked the waitress with a tip and a nod. I ate quickly and got up hoping Sam would not see me. Just as I reached the door, I felt a hand on my shoulder.

"Drew, please…" Sam whispered.

"Sam, I do *not* want to hurt you." I turned to face him. Tears ran down my face. He wiped them away for me. I gave a grim smile.

"Let me help you work through this, Drew. I love you, and I am positive you were not in your right mind when you did that." He kissed me softly.

I kissed him back. "Sam, it is not that easy." I looked away. "I love you, but I just don't want to risk hurting you, or worse, killing you."

"It is that easy." He said matter-of-factly.

"No, Sam. It is not that easy. You are asking me to put the person I love more than anything at risk. I just cannot do that to you, or myself. I cannot lose you like that." And then, I left him standing in the door way of the bar. I ran upstairs to my little room and locked the door, just in case he tried to follow me.

I sat there, on that poorly made bed, and wondered how he had tracked me down. I was well over one thousand miles from his place. More importantly, why would he track me down? I killed someone, for who knows what reason. How on earth could he still want to be with me? I knew the answer. Of course, the answer would be because he is in love with me, and the saying goes, "people do crazy things when they are in love." But this is beyond crazy, this is signing your own death warrant. I have no clue why I killed Isabelle, no way of knowing it will not happen again. And he wants to be with me still. It scares me so much, knowing that he would still willingly be with me, even though I could accidently kill him too. He is everything to me, and I want more than anything to be with him, I am just scared of hurting him in that gone forever way. I know it would kill me emotionally if I hurt him like that. A knock at the door interrupted me.

"Drew, please open the door. I only want to help you. I understand if it means you cannot be with me, but please let me help you."

"Sam, how can you be okay with the fact that I killed her?" I cried. There was no way to stop the raw emotion this time. I opened the door and stood there as he hugged me to his chest and told me everything would be okay.

"Drew, I am not okay with it. It scares me that you did that, but I know you would not normally do that, so there is no way you consciously did it. I need to know what caused you to black out, and murder her. I need to know that the creature who killed her is not my Drew. Do you understand that Drew? Please tell me you understand that."

"I understand that Sam. I just cannot lose you like that. I love you more than I ever thought possible, and you mean everything to me. Do you understand that I just cannot risk your life?" I bit my lip trying to hold back the second wave of tears.

"Drew, you cannot do this on your own. How are you going to figure out why you blacked out all by yourself? You cannot. It is not possible. Not when you have so much going on in your mind right now. So just stop being so dang stubborn and let me help you." His dominating voice is so attractive, I could not help but give in even though I did not want to.

"Okay, Sam. You can help." I hugged him tightly, secretly glad that he had tracked me down and talked me in to letting him help me. We closed the door and sat down on my bed. He had a bag on one shoulder and put it down, pulling out a notebook and pencil.

"We will make a list of possible causes for blacking out. We will test each one to see if it was the cause or not. We already know it was not alcohol so we will not even bother putting that on the list." He turned to a fresh page and paused.

"What?" I looked at him worriedly.

"I started thinking about how the last time I made a list for something; it was about whether or not I should tell you how I feel." He laughed softly. I smiled at him and hugged him gently.

"Let's get this over with." I sighed. We spent the next three hours listing all of the possible causes of making me black out. These ranged from a sinister other personality, to a tumor pressing on my brain. I honestly think the other personality theory makes the most sense. It would also explain killing her, whereas the tumor would not. "How do we test these? I mean, I am sure that the Ashland Police Department figured out I did it by now so we cannot really just walk in to a doctor's office or a hospital." I looked down at my lap nervously.

"I have a psychology degree. I can test you for Dissociative Identity Disorder. If that is what it is, we will know you have another personality. If it is not, we will figure out the rest later." He put his arm around me in a comforting way.

"Okay, let's do it." I was not looking forward to any test of any kind; I just wanted to get it over with.

"Alright, so there are twenty-eight questions that I need you to answer for me." I did as he asked and he tallied my answers. "Drew, I am highly confident in this. I believe you have Dissociative Identity Disorder. I believe that your other personality is the one who killed her, which would explain why you do not remember doing it." Sam's voice was very professional, as if I was a patient of his, not his best friend and possibly his boyfriend.

"Which means it is even more of a risk for us to be together Sam. If he killed her, he could do the same to you." I whimpered softly in to my hands.

"Drew, I love you, and I'm not going anywhere. I know the signs now that I know that I am looking for D.I.D. You and me against the world, right?" He grinned at me as he lifted my head. I smiled back and nodded. I truly do love him. "Good. Now, let's go do something, as boyfriend and boyfriend." He kissed me gently.

"Does this mean you are asking me out, Sir Sam?" I teased.

"Yes, it does. Now, you better not say no, or I will have to beat you up." He punched my arm teasingly.

"I would love to be your boyfriend, Sam. Now, let's go see a movie. My treat, babe." I grabbed his hand and got up, leading him to the door. We left my rented room and went down the road to the theatre. Knowing Sam's taste in movies, I picked the comedy and ordered two tickets. We went and got our seats at the top of the theatre.

He asked if I wanted anything to drink, and went to the concession stand. He came back and we watched in silence, holding hands the entire time. After the movie, we went out to a nice sit-down restaurant for dinner. He gushed about when we first met in the sixth grade and how he thought I was so cute in that button-up shirt. I blushed and smiled. I love watching him get excited about little things like this. It is seriously the cutest thing ever and his eyes light up when he does it.

"Baby, did I ever tell you just how cute you are?" I asked as our food arrived.

"Nope." He grinned. His smile is so sexy.

"Well, take the cutest puppy you have ever seen, multiply that by one hundred million, and it still would not compare to you." I smiled and took a bite of food.

He blushed brightly, half hiding his face with his hand as he toyed with his food before taking a bite. "Babe, you are so totally lying to me."

"Like hell I am. Sam, baby, you are the only guy I have ever had feelings for, let alone slept with. You are so amazing, and I am so lucky to have you in my life, especially as my boyfriend." Now, it was my turn to gush, but I could not help it. My baby deserves to be told how amazing he is every day, and I will be darned if I am not the one telling him it.

"Aww, baby, I love you so much." He teared up a little bit.

"I love you too Sammy-baby." I smiled more throughout this dinner than ever before. We finished our meal and I paid for dinner. We headed back to my- no our room and laid on the bed, just holding each other. For the first time in an extremely long time, I was truly happy.

Screaming, I jumped out of the bed, and this stranger's arms. He jumped in surprise, obviously confused as to why I was screaming. "Who the hell are you?" I asked, backing myself in to the nearest corner.

"Drew, it is just me, Sam." He whispered.

"I am not Drew, and I have never met you before." My voice got shaky.

"Tell me your name, please." Sam asked softly.

"Nico. My name is Nico." I whispered, afraid of him still. He might do what I accidently did to that girl, but to me. I have no way of knowing that he will not.

"Okay, Nico. I am going to tell you a few things and they might shock you. I know you killed that girl, and I know why you do not remember anything after that drive you took afterwards. Drew, the guy who I have been best friends with since we were kids, has Dissociative Identity Disorder, and you are the other personality. You do not know what is going on when he is in control, which is most of the time. This also means that when you are in control, he has no memory of what happens."

"What does this have to do with me waking up in your arms?" I asked nervously.

"Drew and I are dating, and I fell asleep holding him." Sam blushed.

"Oh…" My mind trailed off, causing my voice to do the same. I have this wicked fanfic story going through my mind, and I really need to get it out. "Do you know where I can get a notebook? I have something I want to write down, but yet keep it private." I looked down. I was not exactly lying. I do not want everyone to know about my obsession with the idea of Harry ending up with Ron instead of Ginny.

"There is a dollar store down the road. I can take you if you want." He smiled at me.

"Yeah, that would be great. Just let me get changed?" I grabbed a clean shirt and pair of jeans. "Uhm, where is the bathroom?" I felt stupid asking but I had to.

"See the door next to you? That is the bathroom." Now I really feel stupid.

I went and changed, and did my bathroom business before leaving. "Okay, let's go." I said before going to the door. We went to the store and got a handful of things, including two notebooks and a package of multicolored pens for me. Sam paid for it all and took me out for breakfast. After we finished, we went back to that too small room above the bar. I went back to my corner and sat on the floor, pulling out my new notebooks and pens. I opened up a notebook and got started.

My eyes got wide as Ron drew nearer to me. I knew this was my chance to make a move on my best friend. His room was being cleaned the Muggle way and he was staying in the spare bedroom with me. I had made all of the sleeping bags and spare mattresses disappear, so Ron asked if he could sleep in the bed with me. He slid in to the bed, laying closer to me than he had to. I turned over on to my side so I was facing him.

"Harry, I have a confession to make. I have had a crush on you since the day you asked my mum how to get on to the platform." I smiled as he confessed this.

"Ron, I have liked you ever since then too. I was afraid you would make fun of me or tell everyone, so I regrettably pretended to like Ginny so I could get closer to you." I kissed him deeply. This is the beginning of my new life and my new relationship. ~

"Nico, did you hear me?" The question pulled me back in to reality.

"What? Sorry, I was in to my writing." I blushed deeply.

"I noticed. I asked what you are writing about. You kind of moaned and I got curious." He blushed.

"Oh, uh, just a fanfic that I am extremely embarrassed by..." I covered the notebook and my lap simultaneously hoping I had not gotten hard just by writing about a kiss.

"I understand Nico. I will not pry." And that was the end of it. Sam went back to sitting on the bed, watching me.

"Sam, do you think that because you are with Drew, it would be okay for us to kiss or do anything? Not that I want to, but because I am just curious about it."

"Uh, I have no idea actually. I have never dated anyone who has another personality or anything." Sam explained, kind of surprised with my question.

"Okay." I shut up, and mentally beat myself up for making Sam uncomfortable. "Sorry for asking such a strange question."

"It is okay Nico. I was kind of curious myself. What do you think about it?"

"Well, he and I share a body, so whatever I do affects him, and vice versa. It would make sense if it was okay for it to happen. But at the same time, I am not him, so it does not make sense because it would kind of be cheating." I sniffled a little, because of my frustration, not because I want to be with Sam.

"Hey, it is okay, do not cry please." Sam came over to me.

"I am not upset. Just frustrated. I will be fine." I said feeling pretty pathetic. After all, I am supposed to be a man right? And men are not supposed to get emotional. If I cannot even do that, no wonder I killed that girl. I am a failure at life for Christ's sake. Hell I do not even have my own body.

"Okay, Nico. Just don't worry too much about it okay?" He smiled at me.

"May I go back to writing now?" I asked, needing to have an escape from this.

"Yeah, just do not work too hard."

Ron wrapped his arms around me, pulling me closer while deepening the kiss further. I moaned softly and ran my hand through his hair. Nothing could be better than this. I broke the kiss and smiled, even though he could not see it. I kissed his jaw gently, and slowly made my way down his body, occasionally nipping the spots I had kissed. When I reached the top of his stomach, I switched to licking my way lower, causing him to moan softly.

He stopped me just before I reached his wand. "What is wrong Ron?" I asked nervously.

"I do not want to risk moving too fast Harry," he said nervously. He could act like such a girl sometimes.

"Ron, it's not going to end badly. I promise." I kissed just above his wand. "Let me make you feel good, Ron." I whispered before kissing his wand. He moaned softly, and I took that as his permission to continue. I took his wand in my mouth and gently sucked on the top. One of Ron's hands moved to my head and gripped a handful of hair. I pulled more of it into my mouth, moaning as he pulled at my hair.

"Harry, stop." He whispered, panting a little, "If you turn around I can please you at the same time. Something the Muggles call 69, I believe." I turned so we could please each other simultaneously.

"Nico, come here." Sam's voice called from the bathroom.

"Yeah?" I asked as I opened the door.

"I want to try something." He looked at me. "Maybe it will not be anything like cheating." He pulled me close, and looked me over. "And, it looks like you want to try too."

I blushed. "No, uhm...writing...characters got naughty."

"It doesn't matter. You need relief." He kissed me hard and unzipped my jeans, causing my member to ache with need, I moaned softly and bit his lip. He moaned and lowered my jeans, causing me to moan in response. If we were going to do this, I needed to be complete control of the situation. I licked his lower lip, and he let me in. Kissing Sam was better than anything I have ever imagined before. I broke the kiss.

"Lower my boxers Sam." I whispered in to his ear, nipping at his neck in the process.

"Nico, I am supposed to be in control." He whined at me in between moans.

"Listen Sam, you will do as I say or you will be punished for it, Understand, pet?" He nodded and did as he was told to do. "Good boy, now treat me as if my member were the best lollipop on the planet."

He moaned softly as he sank to his knees. He gently licked the head, causing me to mirror his moans. I put my hand on his head, partially to pet him, but also to stabilize myself better. He licked his way down my shaft. I groaned in pleasure and leaned back to rest against the door; he looked up at me, his eyes meeting mine, and stared. I moaned again, this was easily the most pleasure I have ever received out of life, not just sexually, but in general. He pulled the head of my member in to his mouth, sucking on it gently, but in a needing way. I moaned again, and held his head in place. Carefully, I started thrusting deeper in to his mouth, the top of the head hitting the entrance of his throat.

We both moaned; his moans sending vibrations through my shaft. I sped up slightly, moans increasing, as his tongue lapped at the underside of my hardness. I stopped thrusting as I came. "Crap, I was going to warn you." He pulled my member out of his mouth, stood back up, and showed me that his sexy mouth was filled with my cum. I grinned. "Swallow pet." He moaned and swallowed my load. I kissed him softly, licking my cum off of his lops. "That was amazing, Sam."

"Thank you." He blushed and looked down.

"My turn." I grinned and pushed him against the door. I kissed him as I unzipped and lowered his pants. He bit my lip causing me to moan. I lowered his boxers and slowly broke the kiss, and then I looked into his eyes to find that he was begging me with them. I nodded and kissed my way down his body. I licked the head of his member and he moaned.

"Please, just blow me already, Nico." His voice was soft but needy. I moaned softly, and did as he asked. I gently sucked on his head. I took more in my mouth, and slowly started blowing him. With each moan he gave, I either sped up or took more of him in my mouth until he hit the back of my throat. He grabbed my head, "I'm about to cum, Nico." I relaxed my throat, allowing his member to slip in to my throat as he exploded, moaning with him as I swallowed his cum. He pulled me up and kissed me gently.

"Definitely not cheating?" I asked breaking the kiss.

"Definitely not." He said pulling me towards the bed. "You guys have the same body, and while you may not be the same person, you are very similar."

"Sam, I think I am falling for you…" I looked at my lap.

"Nico, I would have been surprised if you had said otherwise. A lot of people go through the same thing when they have D.I.D." He lifted my head.

I kissed him deeply, wanting more of this man. "Sam, I need you. Please." I begged as I bit at his neck. He pulled away and went to his bag, pulling out a condom and a bottle of lube. I bit my lip in anticipation.

"Nico, turn around for me." He commanded as he put the condom on. I turned around and laid my head down on the bed. It was not long until I felt the cold of the lube on my hole. "This will hurt a little," he said softly while grabbing my hips. He gently pushed the head in, causing me to wince a little. He stopped, allowing me to get used to it before continuing to push in.

I moaned and once he was fully in, I got used to his length. He slowly pulled out, beginning to thrust. I moaned softly and pushed back, causing him to moan as well. "Christ, Nico. Don't stop doing that!" He moaned and pulled out again, thrusting slightly faster but I obeyed all the same.

"Oh god, Sam! This is amazing!" I moaned as I pushed back. Each time his hips met mine it was more amazing than the time before it. Each thrust got a little fast, or a little deeper, or a little harder. And each thrust earned him another moan from my lips. "Oh god. Sam, I am about to cum!" I moaned loudly as my member began to jerk.

"Me too!" Sam thrust in once more and held himself there as we both came. Mine shot across the bed, hitting the wall. His filled the condom, both of us crying out in ecstasy, repeating each other's names over and over again, until we collapsed on the bed, panting wildly. He pulled the condom off and disposed of it before laying back down next to me. I curled up in his arms and we both drifted off to sleep.

6

I awoke in Sam's arms, completely undressed. I have no memory of yesterday whatsoever. I got up and grabbed an oversized t-shirt to throw on. I went to the bathroom and showered, throwing on the t-shirt when I got out. I walked back over to the bed and noticed Sam was still sleeping. "Baby, get up." I said softly as I kissed him.

"Mmm. I am awake. But I have to ask, so do not get mad, are you Drew or Nico?"

"Drew. I guess now I know why I do not remember yesterday. His name is Nico?" I questioned.

"Yeah. Also, we, him and I, came to the conclusion that it is not cheating if he and I do things, because in essence, he is you..." Sam's voice trailed off.

"You slept with him?! Is that why I woke up naked?" I ran to the bathroom and slammed the door, sitting in front of it so he could not get in.

"Drew, please. Baby, let me in." He begged from the other side of the door.

"He murdered her. And you slept with him." I cried, burying my head in my lap.

"Baby, please..." Sam cried. Great, now I get to feel like crap for two things.

"Tell me, Sam. How did it feel knowing that he is not me?" I choked out.

"Drew, how could I stop myself? I was staring at you, only the person inside was not you. Please open up and let me explain."

"Why? So I can feel even worse? Sam just leave me alone for a while."

"Fine...but could you come out? I have to use the bathroom. Please?" I got up and opened the door, lowering my head so I would not have to see how hurt he was. I sat in a corner, feeling more than just pathetic. Sam was right, it technically is not cheating, but it hurts a lot to know that he slept with my other personality. I could not help but feel betrayed. Sam came out of the bathroom and sat on the other side of the room, in the corner farthest from me.

"I... Sam, I am sorry. It's just, I feel betrayed, and even though it is not cheating, I wish you would have talked to me first." I cried as I said this. He came over to me and pulled me close to his chest.

"Baby, I'm sorry too. And you are right; I should have asked you about it. But I had no clue how long it would be until you had control again." He sniffled.

"You still should have waited so you could talk to me about it." I knew I was being stubborn, but I could not help it. Even though I knew I was fine with it happening, I still wanted to know he respects me enough to talk to me about this kind of thing.

"I know, Drew. I am sorry. I should also tell you, like with most people who suffer from D.I.D., Nico has fallen for me. I told him I was not surprised he had, but did not tell him how I feel. I think I love both of you, and if you are okay with me telling him that, I will. But you will always come first." He looked down.

"Sam, you can tell him. Just please talk to me about this kind of stuff first. Okay?" I lifted his chin, kissing him softly.

"Okay Drew." He smiled at me. I pulled him closer to me and held him for a long time. I hated the fact that I had upset him, and I hope that I would not do it again for a very long time. "Does this mean you forgive me?" He asked, hope lacing his words.

"Of course, baby. I think we both know I could never stay mad at you." It was true, I could not. But I guess love would do that to you. "Let's go get some food." We got up and decided to just go downstairs, instead of some fancy place. After all bar food is just as good.

After eating, we went back upstairs to our tiny room. I asked Sam to tell me about Nico. From what Sam has told me, he is a lot like I am; quiet, shy, and tending to keep to himself. And he likes to write. I guess his own story got him hard and that is part of what lead to them sleeping together. Which now, I can understand why it happened. And even though I was getting jealous that Nico had been with him, I was okay with it.

I pulled Sam closer without saying a single word. Kissing him softly, I moved us so we were laying down. I just wanted to be next to my boyfriend, laying side by side. Sex didn't matter to me, just physically being close. I pulled him on top of me, kissing him more passionately than before. I was madly in love with this man.

"Drew…" Sam whispered.

"Yeah baby?" I whispered back.

"If you are not going to take this further, please stop teasing me."

I blushed deeply. "Sorry baby."

He laid down beside me, putting his head on my chest. This felt right, like it was meant to be. "Baby, I love you so much. You mean everything to me." He whispered in to my neck as he raised his head so he could kiss me.

"I love you too, baby. You're my world, my everything; the sun to my world, the bark to my trees. The water to my ocean, and the ever to my for. Don't ever leave me." I sounded so sappy.

"Are you proposing?" He jumped up.

"Uhm…maybe?" I sat up and opened up my bag and pulled out a box. His eyes widened.

"I swear to god if you bought me a ring…" His voice faded out as I opened the box to reveal a charm bracelet. "Drew, you didn't."

"I did." I put the bracelet on his left wrist. "Look, I know it is way too soon to be proposing or even thinking about it, but I love you so much, and I have never been so sure about anything in my life. Not even Isabelle." I blushed and stared in to his eyes.

"Baby, you are amazing. I love you more than you could ever know. I will always wear this with pride. Thank you for the gift babe." He kissed me softly. "You are everything to me."

I teared up at his mini speech. "Aww, baby. I am glad you like it, because I bought it before leaving home, on my way home from work."

"Baby! When were you planning on giving it to me? Or even bringing any of this up?"

"When the Isabelle thing blew over, but obviously that is not going to happen any time soon." I looked down.

"Baby, you deserve the very best. You deserve to be told how amazing you are, how much you mean to me, and so much more every day. There are going to be days where I am going to be stretched thin, and forget to tell you. That's why I got you the bracelet, so you would always know how much you mean to me." I looked up at him. "I love you more than words could ever explain, and I want you to know, just how much I care." I kissed him deeply, and it was suddenly like I could not get enough of him or his touch.

We ended up making love again. Now, laying in his arms, I know that I am loved back. Sure someone can say they love you, but you never truly know until they show it. Sam fell asleep, and I am listening to his heartbeat as I lay here thinking. Thinking about how I want Sam in my future, and that I never want to lose him. And that he completes me in ways I never thought were possible. I truly do love him, and I know he loves both me and Nico, and I would not have it any other way.

"Sam?" I ask as I wake up. No answer. The bed was empty, except for me. Panic was setting in. I missed him as it was, Drew had control yesterday, and now he is missing. I got out of bed, looking for a note, anything to say he went out to get breakfast. I found one but it did not say what I had wanted it to.

"If you ever want to see Sam again, meet me by the old bookstore at noon. ~ Scott."

Okay, who the hell is this Scott guy, and why did he take Sam? I checked the alarm clock. Oh hell, it is almost noon now. I quickly threw on some clothes, and raced down the stairs of the bar. Rushing outside, I sprinted to the book store, worried about Sam, and wanting to beat the hell out of this Scott guy.

"You came." A rough male voice whispered from the alley beside the book store.

"Where is Sam?" I demanded.

"Patience is a virtue." He turned to leave. "Follow me." Against my better judgment, I followed. "As you have probably guessed, I am Scott. And I am your brother, Drew."

"Actually, I'm not Drew. I'm his other personality, Nico. And what do you mean brother?" I could hardly stop myself from asking more questions.

"When you were born, you had a twin, actually an identical twin, who was taken from your mother. I am that twin." For the first time since I arrived, he showed me his face. My jaw dropped as I noticed he was telling the truth. He was truly identical to me. This is insane.

"Oh my god. So why take Sam?" I bit my lip.

"Because Isabelle was not enough." His voice was edged with ice.

"Are you saying you were the one who killed Isabelle? Not me?"

"I did. And I'll kill Sam too. Why? Because you stole my mother from me. This is my revenge," he smirked.

"That was not my fault. I was raised without knowing you even existed. You cannot get away with this!" I screamed at him. "Tell me where he is!"

"I can, and I will get away with it, as the process has already started. However, I cannot tell you where he is. Good-bye, Nico." He took off towards the river. I broke down, crying, wanting to chase after him, but not having the energy to do so. In a fit of rage, I punched the wall next to me. I was angry at Scott for doing this, and angry at myself for not having the courage to chase after him.

I calmed myself down and made myself promise to hunt him down. I followed the last direction I saw Scott head in. I walked along the river, asking people if they had seen anyone who looked like me. I kept following their directions, feeling a bit like a detective, until I got to an abandoned "mom and pop" local store.

I cautiously entered the store, looking around every corner. And then I heard the buzzing of what sounded like an electric razor. I followed the sound, hoping he was only giving Sam a crappy haircut.

"Drew, look out!" Sam called out before I could even see him.

"Oh, it is not Drew. It's little Nico to the rescue."

Scott laughed, mocking my intentions

"I am not little, you narcissistic ass!" Oh hell, I just swore. *This is not the time to be concerned with that,* I scolded myself.

"Poor Nico, no clue where I really am with his little boyfriend, all tied up and ready to die. Tell him, Sam. Tell him how you feel. Tell him how you do not really love him, but that you love Drew." Scott laughed more.

"It is not true Nico. I do love you, just as much as I love Drew. You guys are my world. But I need you to run. Run away and save yourself, Nico." Sam was crying. I knew I could not just walk away from him when he was in trouble.

"I can't do that Sam. Drew would never forgive me if I did that." It was true, but more importantly, I would not be able to forgive myself if I did that.

"Awww, would you look at that. Nico is going to try to be a hero. How cute is that? Too bad it will not work." Scott was really starting to piss me off with his shit. "Nico, I have a story for you. One that you know part of. Please take a seat." He was mocking a good host. "Or don't. It is your choice." I sat on a box. "Before I start, would you like to say anything?"

"Scott, just tell the damn story so I can come up there and kick your ass." I growled.

"Alright, I am starting. So once there was a young woman who gave birth to twins. But one of these twins was stolen from her. She carried on her life as if it had never happened, raising the other child as if there was no brother. While she did this, the stolen twin was plotting his revenge on his brother."

"Why? It was not his fault the other was taken from their mother!" Sam interrupted. Scott smacked him.

"Shut up Sam! Nico, you care to explain this part before I continue?" I could hear that nasty ass grin spreading across his face in his words.

"Sam, Scott and I are the twins..." I choked out, realizing that Scott was coming clean.

"Very good, Nico. Now, as I plotted my revenge, I was making sure I kept up with the new information. That is how I found out about pretty little Isabelle. Her pleads were like music to my ears as I threw her to the ground. She thought I was Drew, pleading 'Drew, please do not hurt me.' I enjoyed carving her up. When you came across me at the river, I drugged you. I told you the details of the crime, showed you her body, all so you would end

67

up thinking it was you who killed her, when it was really me. When you ran away, I thought my revenge was complete, but then Sam had to chase after you, and I decided to follow. Now, it is time to say good-bye to Sam, Nico."

"You are crazy if you think I am going to let you get away with hurting him!" I shouted and jumped up, running towards the stairs. I heard the switch of the razor turn back on, and I ran harder. As I reached the top, Scott was finishing a shitty-ass haircut. "Sam, I love you." I cried out, as I pulled out a knife with a six inch blade. "Say good-bye Scott." I lunged at him,

"Good-bye, Sam." He thrust a knife in to Sam's chest. "I told you I would get away with it Nico." He laughed, pulling the knife out of Sam's chest, causing Sam to gasp more than the thrust in did. I cried out in anger and frustration. Scott then came towards me, a little too eagerly. I blocked his attack and pushed him up against a wall, shoving my knife in to his chest and twisting it, looking away so I would not have to watch the life drain from his eyes. I ran over to Sam and pulled him in to my lap.

"Sam, talk to me please." I cried as I ripped my coat off and pressed it to his chest.

"It hurts, Nico." His voice raspy.

"I know, baby. I will get you help. I promise." I picked him up bridal style. I struggled down the stairs and out the door. "Someone please help me!" I shouted as I walked out the door.

"Nico, I'm sleepy. Can I close my eyes?" Sam begged, and I wanted more than anything to be able to say yes.

"No baby, you have to stay awake. Please stay awake for me." I cried holding him to me. "If you close your eyes, you will never wake up." A man came running up to us.

"What happened?" He asked me.

"He was stabbed. Please help us." I begged. The man went to get his car.

"Get in." I got in the back seat and held Sam tighter, pressing the coat to his chest again.

"Stay with me, Sam. Please, you have to live." I sobbed.

"Nico, my eyes are closing on their own. I am so sleepy, Nico. Please let me rest just a little." He pleaded with me. I looked down just in time to see his eyes close, and his breathing stop. I lost control of myself.

"We're here." The guy whispered from the front of the car.

"Can you go get someone? Tell them you have a newly dead young man held by his best friend in the back of your car. And that I am not sure my legs can carry me inside." I begged, He ran inside and I cried harder. This cannot be good-bye.

"Sir, you have to give us the body." A female voice registered in my mind.

"I can't. My hands don't work. And he's my best friend, and my boyfriend." I bawled.

"Come on, sir. We'll help you, I promise." She helped my hands let go, and they pulled Sam away from me. She then helped me get out of the car. They sat me on a stretcher as they wheeled Sam away. I watched in shock until they laid me back.

7

I awoke in what appeared to be a private room in a hospital. I checked myself for signs of something that Nico could have done to cause me to end up in the hospital. There were no signs of injury, and no medical charts to tell me what was wrong. Even more suspicious, Sam was not here.

I stumbled out of bed and to the door. I opened the door and headed for the nearest nurse. I tapped her shoulder. "Uhm, Miss, could you tell me why I am here?" I asked slowly, not able to get my mouth to fully cooperate with my head.

"What's your name doll?" she asked sweetly.

"Andrew, but I go by Drew."

"Well, Drew, you were brought in with a Sam fellow. He was deceased, and you were in shock." She told me, sympathy lacing its way into her voice.

"What do you mean? Sam is dead?" I started to shake.

"He was stabbed in the chest. The blade nicked his heart. Come on doll. Let's get you back to your room." She led me back to my bed and laid me down.

"He cannot be gone. He just cannot be." I curled up in to a ball.

"Honey, I get off work in twenty minutes. Would you like me to come stay with you for a little while after I get off?" She held my hand. I nodded. "Okay, doll. I'll see you shortly." She left and I rocked slowly.

20 Minutes Later

The door opened. "Doll, I'm back." The nurse called. I peeked out from under my blanket.

"Hi. You never told me your name." I hid again.

"It's Vanessa. And you never asked for my name, Mr. Drew." She pulled the blanket back and smiled at me.

"I didn't? I thought I had. I am sorry. You must think I am some ass-knob..." I trailed off, looking away.

"I don't think that at all. I think you're a young man who just lost someone really important to him." She turned my head so I was looking at her again. "Can you tell me your relationship with him?"

"He was my best friend, and my boyfriend. He was the only guy I have ever liked, and now he's gone." My lower lip trembled.

"Oh honey, don't cry. It's okay. Nurse Vanessa has you now." She pulled me closer to her body, and I allowed myself to snuggle close. She smiled. "Can I get under there with you, Drew?" I nodded and moved over so she could slide under the blanket and hold me. "Thank you, doll." She held me tightly to her chest.

"I don't know how I'll live without Sam. I was going to marry him someday. This isn't fair. It's not fair!" I screamed into her chest.

"Drew, honey, you have to put yourself back together. You still have to get your statement to the officers tomorrow, okay?" She stroked my hair. I nodded, not quite sure how I'd pull it off when I know nothing of what happened. "Are you hungry? I can go get you some lunch if you are."

"Yes please. Just a sandwich and a soda, if possible." I whispered.

"Anything for you doll." She slid out of the bed and left my room. I laid in bed, staring at the ceiling until she returned with food.

"Thank you, Vanessa." I said a little louder than a whisper, for the first time since we first talked.

"You're welcome, Drew." She handed me my food. We ate in silence, not sure what to say to each other. When she finished her food, Vanessa turned on the T.V. that was mounted to the wall.

"Whoa, I have a T.V. in here?" I asked surprised.

"Yeah. I am a little surprised you did not discover it earlier." She teased.

"I laid in bed and stared at the ceiling until you got back." I blushed.

"Pick a channel." She tossed me the remote. "Oh, and you are really cute when you blush." I blushed more and picked my favorite cartoon channel. She laughed at me. "Are you twenty-two or twelve?"

"Both." I stuck my tongue out at her.

"Hush, Mister! Now slide back over!" She ordered me, and I did it. "Good boy." She slid in next to me, and pulled me close again. I rested my head on her chest as I watched my cartoons. "Drew," she asked softly, "can I do something crazy real quick?"

I looked up at her. "Sure Vanessa." She kissed me softly, and I blushed as I kissed her back.

"Sorry, Drew. I had to kiss you just once. I..."

I kissed her again. I put one hand on her chest, kissing her deeper, needing her touch.

"Don't talk. Go lock the door. I need you Vanessa. I need you badly." I whispered into her ear. She got up and locked the door. As she came back, as she came back, she shed her clothes, leaving only her bra and panties on when she reached the bed. I bit my lip and pulled my hospital gown off.

She crawled over to me. "Are you sure about this?" I nodded and pulled her close, kissing her deeply. She pulled away and kissed her way from my neck to my stomach. I moaned softly as she teased me with her tongue. She looked up at me as she pulled my boxers off. I bit my lip again, quieting a moan. She kissed just above my member, and I moaned again.

"Vanessa, please just fuck me!" I wanted to push her head lower, but I did not want to force her. She took the head in her mouth, causing me to whimper slightly with need. She took me in, and lapped at it, pretending it was a lollipop and not a part of my body.

I moaned loudly, needing more than she was giving me right now. I pulled out of her mouth. "I need you now, Vanessa."

She nodded and unhooked her bra. I bit my lip as her gorgeous tits were revealed to me. I flipped us over, so she was laying on her back with me on top. She smiled at me as I kissed her neck teasingly, before making my way down her body, stopping only to tease each nipple. She moaned softly and put a hand in my hair. I kissed down to her panties and nipped at her panty line.

She moaned again, and squirmed slightly under my touch. I carefully took hold of her panties with my teeth and lowered them. I moaned when I saw her pussy. She was shaven, and very soaked. She wanted me just as much as I wanted her. "Hmm, should I tease you with my mouth or should I just screw you senseless? Hmmm... I think I'll tease you first." I licked at her clit, causing her to moan softly, and grip my hair tighter. I licked at her entrance, teasing her by pushing the tip of my tongue in slowly, but withdrawing it quickly.

"Ugh! You tease! Please just fuck me already!" She yelled at me in frustration.

"Naughty, naughty girl. Not only did you swear, but you're trying to order me around. If it would not

be a punishment to me too, I would stop right now."
I grabbed her bra and her panties. "I am going to restrain your hands now, do you understand why?"

"For swearing and trying to order you around."
Her eyes were large as she said this, but her voice was indifferent. I used her undergarments to tie her hands to the bed. She let out a soft moan.

"Oh, you like this do you? Maybe I should give that pussy of yours a few spankings, obviously you do not take me seriously." I gave her a teasingly scolding look.

"No, please don't do that." She whined at me.

"I think I will. How else will you learn your lesson?" I gently smacked her clit, earning a soft moan. "You will receive five smacks, not including the one you just got. And you will count them out loud." I smacked her pussy lips softly and listened to her mix the number one with her moan. "Good girl, Vanessa." I smiled as I smacked her again.

"Two, sir." She moaned at me, squirming slightly, tugging at her restraints. I smacked her hand and gave her a warning look. She bit her lip, obviously nervous to see if I would make the next one harder. I smacked her again, a little lower so the tip of my middle finger parted her pussy lips. "Three, sir." She tried to resist moaning, but failed. I grinned, and smacked her again. "Four, sir." She bit her lip once again.

"This one will be the hardest." I smacked harder, causing my finger to slip inside her.

"Five, sir." She moaned, looking me in the eye. I moved back up, and kissed her gently. While I kissed her, I lined myself up at her entrance. I softly bit her lip. When she moaned, I slipped inside her, causing her moan to get louder. I took my time speeding up for my pleasure, sometimes giving in to her pleas. Every five to ten thrusts, I would thrust harder or deeper, alternating which it was. For once, sex was great, and kept my mind busy. I was enjoying being in control when she could cum, and when I would shoot my own load inside her. "Oh god! I'm gonna cum!" she screamed out.

"Me too!" We came together and I untied her.

"Oh my god, that was amazing." Vanessa panted as I laid down next to her.

"Yeah, it was." I closed my eyes. "You should get dressed and leave now. Before anyone finds out you slept with me, you know, a patient." I was being a total douche, but I really did not care. All I had wanted was the sex. And that is exactly what I got.

"Oh…yeah…" She sounded like she was going to cry, but I did not care anymore. She quickly got dressed, unlocked the door, and left. Finally, some peace. I quickly drifted off to sleep.

I woke up several times through the night, crying after dreaming about Sam. How Drew was coping with this, I had no idea. All I can see is Sam's face draining of color as I hold him. This is torture. I threw on a clean gown just as someone knocked on my door. I opened it to a pair of officers.

"How are you feeling?" The taller officer asked me.

"Like, shit, honestly. My best friend died in my arms after I had to fend off my long lost twin brother by killing him before he killed me." I rubbed my eyes out of morning habit.

"We understand. We just need your statement." The other one said sympathetically.

"He kidnapped Sam and left a note asking me to meet him by the old book store. I did, and he told me that he was the one who killed my ex-girlfriend, and that he was going to kill Sam too. I followed him to the abandoned store on the river where he told Sam and I his life story. He then began to attack Sam and I pushed him away from Sam, but it was too late, he had already been stabbed by Scott. In a fit of rage, I stabbed Scott before he could get me. Then I carried

Sam out of the store and found someone to help us get here, but Sam died in my arms as we pulled up." My voice cracked several times.

"Thank you. Wait, you said your brother Scott was the one who killed your ex? Would that be the girl from Ashland?" The first officer asked.

"Yes, sir." I bit my lip nervously, hoping they would not going to arrest me.

"The locals tried to contact you saying they knew who it was, but you never showed up at home." I turned red.

"I thought I had done it, but Scott had drugged me and brainwashed me in to thinking that." I looked down.

"When you get out of this hospital, we will take you to the bar where you are staying, and can escort you home to help you make arrangements for Sam's funeral if you would like." The second officer offered.

"Sure, someone needs to do it. Uhm, Scott's body, is it still at the store?" I bit my lip, hoping they had taken care of it already.

"No, we recovered it, and notified his legal family of his death. They did not seem surprised that he had gotten himself killed by attacking someone though, which makes us think he has always been a troubled kid." The officers said their good-byes and left. I was released the next day, and they followed through with the offer.

I made Sam's funeral arrangements and prepared myself to say my final farewell to my best friend and my boyfriend.

THE AUTHOR

Ever since elementary school Jace has always loved
writing, and while in high school became a published
poet. And ever thankful for the teachers who helped
introduce and seek out those opportunities, Jace plans to
pay it forward for other up and coming writers.

Jace Avery originally hails from the state of Michigan,
and shares quarters with a pit bull mix that is as
beloved as any child.

48775017R00052

Made in the USA
Lexington, KY
12 January 2016